BRIGID LUCY

Wants NEEDS a Friend

Leonie Norrington

Illustrated by Tamsin Ainslie

LITTLE HARE

www.littleharebooks.com

Little Hare Books
an imprint of
Hardie Grant Egmont
85 High Street
Prahran, Victoria 3181, Australia

www.littleharebooks.com

Text copyright © Leonie Norrington 2013

Illustrations copyright © Tamsin Ainslie 2013

First published 2013

National Library of Australia
Cataloguing-in-Publication entry

Norrington, Leonie.
Brigid Lucy needs a friend / written by Leonie Norrington ;
illustrated by Tamsin Ainslie.
978 1 921894 24 4 (pbk.)
Norrington, Leonie. Brigid Lucy ; 3.
For primary school age.
Friendship—Juvenile fiction.
Ainslie, Tamsin, 1974-
A823.3

Cover design by Vida & Luke Kelly
Set in 13/19 pt Stone Informal by Clinton Ellicott
Printed by WKT Company Limited
Printed in Shenzhen, Guangdong Province, China, May 2011

5 4 3 2 1

This product conforms to CPSIA 2008

Contents

*To Josephine Marie Izod, who inspired
the character Matilda—LN*

*For my brother, Luther, who was always
my best friend when I needed one—TA*

Prologue

Hello. You're a reader, aren't you? Do you know who I am? I'm the Brigid Lucy storyteller person thing. I tell all the stories about me and my **best friend**, Biddy.

Am I an imp?

No way! Of course I'm not an imp.

If I was an imp I would look like this . . .

   Or this . . .

But I don't. **Slip sloppy Goolag**. I would never want to have fluffy wings or long toenails.

If I was to look like anything, I would look like this . . .

Or this . . .

Now let me tell you the story . . .

How did me and Biddy become best friends?

Biddy used to live on a farm and I lived in the **Great Bushland** that spread out way beyond infinity all around the farm. One day, I was playing in a gum tree when I heard a loud sob. I got such a fright, slipped and tripped and **plonk!** I landed in Biddy's hair. She was crying, 'I'm not going away,' she sobbed. 'I'll never find a friend in the city.'

'Do you want a friend?' I said running out to the end of her nose. 'I do too. I've wanted a friend for a million years. Can I come to the city and be your friend?'

But she ignored me and kept on crying.

2

That's when I realised that she couldn't see me or hear me. So I climbed into her hair and became her 'best friend' all by myself.

And we've had the most exciting adventures. One time we went to a pet shop and I flew on a parrot. Another time we went into a princess tower. An evil wizard had turned a princess into a huge copper bell and locked her up. We helped her escape.

I totally love being Biddy's best friend.

But Biddy doesn't like being my friend. She wants a human best friend. One who is popular. (*Popular* is like if you have a new car, or a pony like Annabelle, or do ballet with soft shoes and glitter like Sascha.) When Biddy first came to the city, she tried to get a friend at school. But Annabelle was Vanessa's best friend, Sascha was Padula's best friend. And Molly and Alice had each other. There were no friends left for Biddy. So Biddy made a plan to find a friend outside of school, during the holidays.

But Biddy's mum is 'expecting-again' (which is like getting really fat). So she doesn't want to go out. All she ever does is cleaning and washing and cooking. And looking after Biddy's little sisters Miss Getting-All-The-Attention Matilda and Crybaby Ellen.

I don't care. I love staying home and playing imagination games. But Biddy says, 'I'll never find a best friend if I stay home the whole of the school holidays.'

'Biddy, darling,' Mum says, 'I said we could go to the Botanic Gardens on Friday. Dad is taking the day off to come with us.'

Me and Biddy love the Botanic Gardens. It is the most magical enchanted place in the whole city. But Friday is nearly a year away.

So Biddy says, 'Can't we go today?' And when Mum says 'no' Biddy yells, 'You don't care if I never get a friend.' And she bursts into tears. 'You are the meanest, horriblest mother in the world.'

Mum says, 'Brigid-Lucy-don't-be-rude!'
And, 'You-need-time-out.' And, 'Go-and-sit-
quietly-in-your-room-for-ten-minutes.'

'How can I find a friend in a locked-up
bedroom prison?' Biddy yells, and throws
herself on her bed. 'I wouldn't be rude if
you let me get a best friend.' Then she puts
her face in the pillow. 'I will never find a
friend, **never ever**.'

I do feel sorry for Biddy. But I don't want
her to get a human friend. What if she
gets one that hates imagination games
like Jamie next door? Or hates reading like
Annabelle? Or says, 'No you can't play with
us,' or, 'You're not my friend anymore' stuff,
like Bree?

'Come on Biddy,' I say, 'forget about best
friends. Let's play **pirates** with ships full
of treasure. Let's fight fabulous sea monsters
with whiskers like octopus tentacles and
nineteen different coloured legs.'

But she ignores me and sucks her
thumb.

'Fine,' I say stomping back into her hair.

'Be boring, then. I don't want to be your friend when you do boring sucking thumb stuff.'

So that's the problem. (You know how all stories have a problem? Well that is the problem for this story.) Biddy wants to find a silly human friend and I want her to play with me—her already best friend.

Shall I tell you that story? Okay. Wait— I have to start it properly . . . I'll just stand up here on the top of Biddy's head like a real storyteller.

Are you listening?

'Long ago, before the dawn of time . . .'

No, I can't say that because it is happening right now . . .

'One day,' I start again, 'there was a little girl called Biddy. Her evil parents had locked her in a bedroom prison. Biddy was so sad. But her invisible friend (that's me) . . .'

'Am I boring?' Biddy interrupts. 'Is that why I haven't got a best friend?'

'Shh, Biddy,' I say. 'I'm telling a story.'

'If I was a **pirate** I wouldn't be boring,' Biddy says, jumping off her bed.

'Biddy, stay still,' I yell. But it's too late. She is running and I'm slipping. I grab a handful of hair and swing out behind her. 'Wait,' I yell. 'You are getting into the story without me.'

Chapter one
pirates and pigsties

'I need a pirate costume,' Biddy says, tipping over her toy box and rummaging through the toys. 'Ah-ha! My dagger!' She spins around with her dagger in her hand, threatening all the other pirates on the pirate ship. 'Now, where is my pirate hat?'

'**Craaark!**' I yell. A pirate's best friend is a parrot. So I'm on Biddy's shoulder being her best pirate parrot friend.

'**Ahh-ha!**' Biddy snarls. She runs to her cupboard, pulls out a drawer and grabs a hat. It is white with pink flowers. It is not very piratey.

'**Nah!**' Biddy says, throwing the hat over her shoulder.

She pulls out a green cap. 'Nah!'

An orange one. 'Nah!'

Finally she pulls out the drawer and tips it upside down.

'**Craaark!** That one!' I say, pointing with my beak to a purple sun hat.

She puts it on, turns up the edges and runs to her mirror. 'That's better,' Biddy says. 'Now I need a one-eye.' She grabs a headband and wraps it around her head so it covers one eye.

'**Aarrr!**' she growls into the mirror, holding her dagger up like a fierce pirate. She looks a tiny bit like a pirate.

'I am the Captain Brigitte Loos,' she yells into the mirror. 'The fiercest captain on all of the vast oceans. My best friend is Princess Isolde who lives in a castle on the sheer black cliffs of Bittangabee Bay.

'I have killed the giant sea dragon and stolen his **treasure**.' Biddy walks to her new bunk beds. 'I am taking the treasure in my ship to my friend Princess Isolde.' She climbs to the top bunk, pulls out her imaginary telescope and looks out to the horizon.

'**Land ahoy!**' I yell in a pirate
parrot voice, pointing out the window
with my wing.

'Land ahoy!' Biddy yells. 'All hands on
deck!' she tells her pirate crew.

'See, Biddy,' I say. 'We don't need a **silly**
human friend.'

Suddenly the door opens. 'What is all
this noise about?' Mum asks.

'No!' I yell. 'Don't interrupt us now. This
is the first fun we've had all year.'

Mum looks into Biddy's room. She sees

the clothes flung about, the drawers upside down, the toys and games all over the floor. 'Brigid Lucy,' she says. 'What are you doing?'

'Biddy's naughty, hey, Mum?' Miss Getting-All-The-Attention Matilda says.

'I am not,' Biddy says. 'I was just practising to be a best friend pirate.'

'Brigid, I asked you to play quietly and look what you have done,' Mum says. 'This room is a pigsty.'

'It is not a pigsty,' Biddy says. 'Pigsties have mud, pigs and . . .' and for a moment she can't think what else pigsties have. Then she remembers, '. . . and they have lots of stinky, **pooie** piggy smells.'

'Stop-arguing,' Mum says. And, 'Clean-up-this-room.' She tries to bend down to pick up a toy but her belly is too fat. So she puts Ellen on the floor and sits down to pick up the toys and put them in the toy box.

'Mum,' Biddy says, jumping down from the top bunk. 'You're ruining my games.' She holds Mum's hand. 'Everything is **perfect**. This is the palace garden. Those are the cliffs of Bittangabee Bay. I am a best friend pirate.'

'Biddy, darling,' Mum says, 'when you finish a game you have to put your toys away.'

'But I'm not finished,' Biddy says. 'None of these games are finished.'

'A game is finished when you stop playing,' Mum says.

Which is totally **ridiculous**. Games

are like stories. They are never finished. But Mum doesn't care. She changes the subject.

'You can't have a friend stay over if your room is messy,' she says.

'A friend stay over?' Biddy says, her eyes bright with excitement. 'Could I really have a friend stay over?'

'Of course you can, darling,' Mum says.

'Biddy, don't listen to her,' I say. 'You can't have a friend stay over if you don't even have a friend.'

But Biddy ignores me and helps Mum pick up the toys and tidy the room.

'Look, Mum, I'm good helping,' Matilda says picking up Biddy's **magic** silver wand.

'Matilda, you are not allowed to play with my special things,' Biddy says, trying to take the wand off her.

'I am so,' Matilda screams, snatching the wand behind her back. 'I'm allowed to help! Hey, Mum!?' really loud.

This makes little Ellen start to cry.

Even though Ellen can walk and doesn't need a nappy, she still cries all the time.

Mum cuddles little Ellen and says, 'Shhh, shhh,' while she picks up the rest of the toys. Then she stands up and says, 'Come on, Matilda, time for a rest.'

'I'm not tired,' Matilda yells.

Mum picks up Matilda in her spare arm and tells Biddy, 'You are to play *quietly* in your room. You can read. You can have a rest. But you are not to pull your toys out and mess this room up again. Do you understand?'

'Don't worry, Mum,' Biddy says, 'I'm keeping my room spotless for my best friend girlfriend to come over.'

'Good girl,' Mum says and walks out.

We can hear Matilda yelling, 'I'm not even tired.' And, 'I'm a big girl,' all the way down the hall.

Biddy lies down on her bed and smiles around her sucking thumb. 'I'm going to have a best friend stay over,' she whispers.

'Come on, Biddy. Let's do something,' I say. 'Let's . . . Let's . . .' I look around. Up on the shelf is a crystal ball. It used to be a goldfish bowl, but the goldfish ate too much and got sick. It is round and glass just like a crystal ball. I run onto Biddy's sucking thumb and tell her, 'Let's play with the crystal ball. You can be a **wicked wizard** looking into the future.'

Chapter two
wizards in trouble

Biddy's eyes look straight past me to the goldfish bowl. 'What a **splendiferous** idea,' she says jumping up. She gets the goldfish bowl down and puts it on the floor.

'I will look into the future and find my best girlfriend in this magic crystal ball.'

She gets her torch, a bottle of glitter and her magic silver wand. Then she pulls the sheet off her bed to make a cape and closes the curtains so no sunlight gets through. Her bedroom is as dark as a scoriak cave.

Scoriaks come from the Great Bushland where I come from. They are older than the earth and they know magical Incantation Songs that can turn you into a piece of **infinity**.

But this is not a real scoriak's cave. So I am not scared. Not one little bit.

I stand on Biddy's shoulder. She sits down beside the crystal ball and puts the torch in her lap so it shines up under her chin. The light makes her face go old and wrinkly. She waves her silver wand above the bowl, then drops **glitter** to sparkle like lights of electricity above the crystal ball.

'Brigid Lucy,' Biddy says, glaring into the bowl with her eyes big and round, 'you are a princess with long hair and ribbons on her shoes.'

She closes her eyes and shakes her head, then opens them again. 'I can see Princess Brigid at the Botanic Gardens,' she says in her wizard's voice. 'I can see Princess Brigid throwing her frisbee through the air,' she pauses. 'Then out from the trees comes another princess on a white horse. Her name is **Isolde**. She gallops up and catches Brigid's frisbee. Then she throws it back to Princess Brigid and they become best friends forever.'

'An imaginary princess friend?' I say. 'That's a great idea, Biddy. Imaginary friends are the best. They are never boring or horrible.'

There's a knock at the door. 'Diddy?' a voice calls.

It's Matilda.

'What you doing?' she says and opens the door, letting light into the room and blink! the magic crystal ball turns into a **boring** old fish bowl.

'Now look what you've done, Matilda,' I yell. But she can't hear me so she just says, 'Diddy, can I play?'

'Matilda, go back to Mum,' Biddy says.

'Mum's asleep,' Matilda says.

It used to be that, in the afternoon, Mum would put Matilda and little Ellen to sleep then do 'quality time' stuff with me and Biddy. We'd do cooking and painting and talking. But now Mum is 'too-tired'. She lies down 'for a rest' too. Sometimes she stays there till Matilda and Ellen wake up. And now she's asleep when Matilda is awake!

The rule is that *Little-kids-are-not-allowed-to-be-up-by-themselves-because-what-if-the-house-catches-on-fire*. But sometimes Mum does ask Biddy to play with Matilda. And Biddy doesn't have a friend to play wizards with, and playing with a little sister might be better than with no one at all.

So Biddy lets Matilda come in. 'We will pretend that you are my best friend,' she says. 'Your name is Isolde and you ride a beautiful white horse.'

'But I can't ride a horse,' Matilda says.

'Then you can have a silver Siamese cat with blue eyes,' Biddy says.

'Okay,' Matilda says. She sits down, picks up her imaginary Siamese cat and starts to stroke it.

Biddy closes the door. The room is dead dark again.

'Biddy, I can't see,' Matilda says her voice quavering.

Biddy turns the torch on. It hits the goldfish bowl and turns it into a crystal ball again.

Slivers of light rush across the room and shadows flicker on the walls. They look like nefariouses dancing. Nefariouses come from the Great Bushland. They are beautiful ancient creatures that dance in the shadows and hate noisy children.

'I'm the Wizard Merlin,' Biddy says in a croaky wizard voice. 'You have come to ask my advice,' she tells Matilda. 'Now, ask me a question.'

Matilda sits up straight and keeps her mouth closed like a big girl.

'Will I tell you your future?' Biddy asks.

Matilda nods.

Biddy puts the torch under her chin. Her face goes old and wrinkly again. She waves her wand over the crystal ball, rolls her eyes back and sings, 'Garrlim. Gooolim. Ambidextrous. Pyrotechnics.'

When Matilda sees Biddy's eyes disappear, her eyes get bigger and bigger. But she doesn't cry. She cuddles her imaginary cat and acts as brave as she can.

'Crystal ball,' Biddy says in her croaky wizard's voice, 'what does the future hold for Isolde?'

Biddy listens while the crystal ball tells her all its secrets.

Then she takes the torch away and tells Matilda, 'You're going to be a mummy.'

Matilda is so relieved to see Biddy's normal face again she smiles. 'Can I be the Easter Bunny?'

'Not a bunny, silly,' Biddy says. 'A mummy like Mum. You can't be the Easter Bunny because he's not real life.'

'The Easter Bunny is so real,' Matilda says her face creasing up.

'He is not,' Biddy says. 'The only things that are real are the tooth fairies and dragons and fairies and ghosts.'

Then, she stands up, lifting her arms up to be a ghost, 'Ohhhhh,' and floats around the room with the torch under her chin. 'I'm a ghost.'

Matilda screams, 'Stop it, Biddy!'

But Biddy can't hear her because ghosts don't have ears.

So Matilda jumps up and screams, 'Mummy!' louder, bashing on the door. Then opening it and running down the hall. 'Biddy's s**caring** me!'

'Oh, Bumble Bee's Bubble. I think I'm in trouble,' Biddy says. 'Do I really look scary?' She looks in the mirror and puts the torch under her chin. And she does! She looks wickedly, monstrously scary. I love Biddy's scary face way past infinity and impossibility put together. Especially when she screws up her mouth and **growls**. This is too much fun.

Until—'Brigid Lucy.' Mum opens the door. 'What did you do to Matilda?'

Biddy quickly pulls the torch away from her face and says, 'Nothing.'

But it is too late, Mum has already seen her wicked wizard face. 'Brigid Lucy!' she yells. 'What-on-earth-are-you-doing?' and snatches the torch from her, pulling Biddy's wizard's cape off. 'What-is-wrong-with-you?

Why did you frighten Matilda? And why have you messed your room up again?'

'I was just playing best friends,' Biddy explains. 'Matilda wanted to play!'

But Mum doesn't listen. She pulls the curtains back and turns our wizard cave into a boring old bedroom again. 'Brigid Lucy,' she says, 'you-are-**incorrigible**.' (That is an adult word meaning very very naughty.) 'You can stay in this room till your father comes home.'

Biddy lies on her bed sucking her thumb. I try to get her to read or play. But she closes her eyes. I feel all **alone** like Biddy isn't my friend anymore. So I go and sit on the windowsill and watch the clouds turn pink and purple as the sun goes down and all the people come home from work.

Chapter three
manners and niceness

After hours and hours, nearly one whole day, Dad comes home. Then Mum and Dad come to Biddy's room. Biddy sits up, pulls her thumb out and tucks it under her pillow so they won't tell her off about being too-old-to-suck-your-thumb.

Mum tells Dad about Biddy being rude. And messing up her room. Twice! And then *deliberately* scaring Matilda 'out-of-her-wits'.

Which is not true. We didn't deliberately scare Matilda. We were just being scary and . . . Anyway, Mum should have been looking after Matilda, not falling asleep and making us look after her when we are only kids.

But Mum doesn't care. She says that
Biddy is 'the-eldest' and needs to be 'a-help'
rather than 'a-hindrance' (which is like a
fence I think). And 'stop-going-out-of-her-
way-to-be-naughty'.

'I didn't go out of my way,' Biddy says.
'I was——'

'Brigid Lucy!' Mum yells. Then she
takes a deep breath and says quietly,
'You have to learn that there are
CONSEQUENCES for your actions.'

'But I wouldn't have played pirates if you
didn't send me to my room,' Biddy says.
'That's the consequence of room-sending.'

'Brigid,' Mum says, telling Biddy to
'be-quiet'.

But Biddy stands up and keeps talking.
'And I wouldn't have played Crystal Balls
except I wasn't allowed to play with my
toys. That's the consequence of no-playing-
with-toys.'

'Brigid Lucy!' Mum yells. Then her face
goes all red and her eyes go watery like she
is going to CRY.

Dad tries to put his arm around Mum to say, 'It's okay.'

But she doesn't listen. She stands up and walks out the door.

Dad looks at Biddy.

Biddy looks at Dad.

Dad says, 'Brigid!' as if he is going to tell her off.

But then he stops.

'Brigid,' he starts again. 'Mum is . . .' then he runs out of words again.

He takes a deep breath and thinks hard.

'Is Mum crying?' Biddy asks, her voice going **croaky**. And thinking about Mum crying makes Biddy's eyes fill up with tears and a big knot fills her throat.

Dad takes another deep breath, then he says all in a rush, 'We will not go to the Botanic Gardens on Friday if you don't start behaving.'

'You can't!' I yell. 'That is not fair. We are going to play **imagination** games at the Botanic Gardens.'

'No Botanic Gardens?' Biddy starts to cry. 'What about my best friend Princess Isolde on her white horse and the **frisbee**?' Tears pour down her cheeks.

'Biddy, don't cry,' Dad says. And, 'Okay we will go.' And, 'Biddy, listen to me.' He holds Biddy's face in his hands. 'We can go to the Botanic Gardens but you have to be good. You have to help Mum.'

Biddy stops crying. 'I do. I will,' she says wiping the tears away. 'I'll help Mum with her jobs.'

Dad lifts his eyebrows.

'I could take little Ellen to the park,' Biddy says.

Dad shakes his head.

'What if I walk to the shop and buy the milk and bread (and perhaps a very small ice-cream).'

'No,' Dad says shaking his head harder.

'Mum would never let me go down the street on my own, would she?' Biddy agrees. 'But I could do it **surreptitious**.' (That's an adult word meaning sneakily.)

'Brigid!' Dad says it like a warning.

'Okay,' Biddy says. 'It has to be something Mum wants me to do.' She pulls her mouth sideways to think better.

'Manners and niceness,' I tell her. 'Those are the only things that Mum likes.'

'I could be nice to Matilda,' Biddy says.

Dad nods his head.

'I could **play** with baby Ellen when Mum is busy.'

Dad nods his head harder.

'And I could smile.' Biddy practises smiling. 'And,' she says, 'I will be very, very **polite**.'

Dad nods his head, holding his smile down in the corners of his mouth.

Biddy stands up tall and does a pretend smile. Then she practises saying, 'Please.' Then, 'Thank you.' And, 'Excuse me.' And finally, she **burps** and says, 'Pardon me.'

Dad laughs big and loud. 'It's a deal then,' he says, taking hold of Biddy's hand. 'You will be good and help Mum.'

He shakes her hand as he says, 'And I will take you to the Botanic Gardens on Friday.'

Why is he shaking her hand? Maybe when they shake hands it binds their words to help them become true.

Dad stands up. 'Now let's go and get our dinner.'

'Yes, Daddy,' Biddy says. Then she says, 'Thank you,' and walks with him down the hall to the dinner table with a very polite smile on her face.

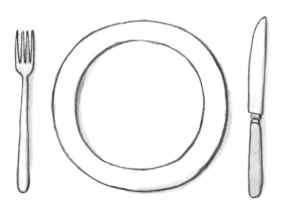

Chapter four
Dad does it wrong

Biddy is so good and polite at dinner. She doesn't talk with her mouth full or **kick** Matilda under the table. She doesn't fiddle, or jump up and down or fill her mouth too full.

But Mum and Dad don't notice. Mum just says, 'Stop-playing-with-your-food,' when Biddy is only trying to find a bit of food she likes.

There is nothing **yummy** to eat, so she asks politely, 'Could I please have fish and chips?'

'Brigid, stop it!' Mum says. 'You are being too silly for words.'

'"Silly" is a word,' Biddy says.

Which is true. But Dad doesn't think so.

'Brigid Lucy,' he says getting up. 'Come and help me stack the dishwasher!'

'Stack the dishwasher? Yes, Biddy, do,' I yell. I **adore** the dishwasher. She is like a special magical helper. Like, you know, the elves in the shoemaker story. How they made the poor shoemaker's shoes for him? The dishwasher is exactly the same, except she can only wash dishes.

Me and Biddy are the best helpers. Dad rinses the plates and Biddy puts them between the wires. The knives and forks have their own little special cage.

'Am I being a **good** girl, Dad?' Biddy asks.

'Yes, you are,' Dad says. 'Put the sharp knives downwards so you don't cut yourself.'

When we are finished, Dad says, 'Good helping, Biddy,' as if he is a teacher.

Then he reaches up to get the special dishwashing powder from the high-up **POISON—DO NOT TOUCH** cupboard.

All the magic get-well potions that Biddy's granny makes and all the poison cleaning bottles have to go up high in there because little Ellen and Matilda might drink them and die **dead**.

Dad pours a little teeny bit of powder into the pocket in the door of the dishwasher. Then he closes the door.

'That is not enough,' I say. 'That tiny bit of powder can't wash all those dishes.'

But Dad doesn't care. He turns the dial and . . . clunk! He tells the magical dishwashing machine to wash the dishes with not enough powder. It's **wrong**. Dad often does things wrong. Like, when he baths us, he doesn't use soap. He just lets us play in the water till the dirt soaks off.

Now he's done the dishwashing wrong.

'Biddy,' I say, 'Dad did it wrong.'

But she ignores me.

I run out onto the end of her nose. 'Dad didn't put enough powder in!' I yell, waving my arms. 'The dishes will come out dirty.'

Still she ignores me.

I run to her ear. 'We have to put in more powder!' I scream as loud as I can.

Just then I hear . . . **Click!** What's that? Biddy is opening the dishwasher. 'Yes! Biddy,' I yell. 'Now put some more dishwashing powder in!'

She looks up at the POISON—DO NOT TOUCH cupboard and shakes her head, remembering that she is not allowed to go in that cupboard.

'Biddy,' I say, 'this is an **emergency**. Sometimes you have to do "not-allowed" things in an emergency.'

But she doesn't. She reaches across the kitchen bench. She picks up the dishwashing detergent off the sink. Good idea. If it can wash dishes in the sink it can wash dishes in the dishwasher.

'Biddy, you are my goodest, bestest clever girlfriend ever,' I say.

Biddy holds the dishwashing detergent with both hands, aims it into the open door of the dishwasher and squeezes.

An arc of detergent squirts into the dishwasher. **Splosh!** All over the plates and cups and knives and forks.

Then she puts the detergent back on the sink and closes the dishwasher. The light comes back on. **Wrrrr! Clink!** The dishwashing machine is happy. She starts washing straightaway.

'See, Biddy,' I say. 'We are the best team. We don't need other friends. We are going to the Botanic Gardens to play imagination. **Yippidyloo!**'

'Mum will be so happy with my helping,' Biddy says and skips on the spot. 'She will buy me a new purple sparkly frisbee,' she says. 'And me and my friend Princess Isolde will spin it through the air like a magical flying saucer. And everyone else at the Botanic Gardens will see us.' Then remembering that she promised to be nice to Matilda, she says, 'And I will give Matilda my old frisbee. It still works, even if it is **pink**.'

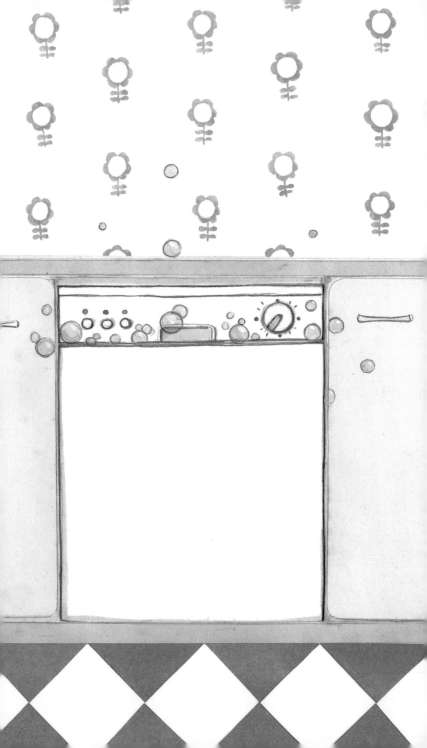

Chapter five

splendiferous bubbles

Look, **bubbles!** You know bubbles?
Those all-round and see-through things,
with rainbows glistening on their skin?
There are hundreds of tiny ones collecting
along the edge of the dishwasher like
foam.

I know all about foam. When there is a
big storm in the Great Bushland the rain
makes humongous waterfalls. They rush
bubbling and foaming over the cliffs. It is
fun to watch.

But you can't swim there. Slivigools like
to wash their hair in this foamy waterfall
water. It makes it **sparkle** with light
and smell like the sun. If you swim there,
the slivigools will wrap their hair around

your legs and pull you under and drown you dead.

But I'm not scared of this foam. This is dishwashing foam, not slivigool foam. I want to dive into it and kick the foamy bubbles up into the air.

Biddy does too. She picks up a handful of bubbles and throws them above her head. They float like sparkling droplets of water.

There's a big bubble. Some of the little bubbles are staying on the dishwasher, growing bigger and bigger, until one by one they let go and float in sparkling colours through the air.

I wish I could go for a **ride** on one of those big floating bubbles.

Biddy wants me to go for a ride, too. She reaches her arm up and catches a huge bubble on her hand.

'Thank you! Thank you, Biddy!' I yell and run along her arm to the bubble. It is beautiful. It's got a whole **rainbow** shimmering on its side.

I touch it.

It's a bit sticky. And soft.

Hey, let go! My hand is stuck to the bubble.

I pull and pull. But I can't get my hand back. I put my foot up to push. No way! Now my foot is stuck, too!

I'm getting sucked into a bubble.

'Biddy!' I shout. 'Help me, please!'

Gulp!

I'm inside the bubble. Everything outside looks strange and huge. Biddy's hand is like a giant's hand. She lifts me up to her face. Her face is all warped. Her eyes are small and her mouth is so big it is like a fillikizard dragon's. She's opening her mouth.

'No! Biddy, don't eat me!' I yell. I close my eyes and cover my head with my hands.

Suddenly the bubble **wobbles**. I open my fingers. And my eyes.

Biddy is blowing. She wasn't going to eat me! She was just blowing the bubble into the air.

I'm floating. In a bubble. I can see the top of the fridge where Dad puts his keys so Matilda can't play with them and lose them.

And there's the inside of the POISON—DO NOT TOUCH cupboard. I can see all the bottles full of magic and poison.

Biddy is far away down below. She looks like . . . well, just like Biddy, but smaller. I float up and **up and up**, until I'm nearly touching the ceiling. Then the bubble hangs in the air for a moment and starts to sink down again.

Biddy slides across the slippery floor, gets under the bubble and blows me up again. I float and stop and start floating down again. 'Biddy, blow at me again!' I yell as my bubble sinks toward her.

She skids across the bubbly floor and blows me up again.

This is **splendiferous** fun.

'Bubbles!' Matilda yells, reaching her arms through the baby rail that keeps her and little Ellen out of the kitchen. Her eyes are wide with excitement. 'Daddy, look. Bubbles in the kitchen.'

'What?' Dad says. 'Where?' He's in the doorway, looking around the kitchen.

I look too. There are bubbles everywhere glistening all over the floor, sparkling on the bench top, floating in the air like tiny silver jewels. They look so **beautiful**.

But Dad doesn't think so. 'Brigid Lucy! What have you done?'

Biddy opens her mouth to explain.

But Dad doesn't listen. He just jumps over the baby rail, and slip! One foot goes left and the other one goes right. He waves his arms. He skips his feet. He skids. He slides and **plonk!** He falls on the floor. **Whack!** He hits his head. **Slump!** He sprawls out on the floor.

'Daddy!' Matilda starts to cry really loud. 'Mummy. Daddy.'

'What's going on?' Mum looks through the doorway and sees Dad on the floor. 'What's happened?' She is climbing over the baby rail telling Matilda, 'It's okay, darling.'

'Don't come in here,' Dad yells, holding his head. 'The floor is slippery.'

Mum looks around the bubbly kitchen. 'How much powder did you put in that dishwasher?' she yells at Dad, her voice very **grumpy**.

'The right amount!' Dad yells back.

'Well, how did this happen?' Mum asks, carefully stepping toward him, one hand on the bench and one on her belly.

'Careful!' Dad says. And, 'Stay there.' He holds his hands up to catch her when she falls. 'What about the baby?'

Baby? What's he talking about? Oh, she means little Ellen! She is in her highchair. I can see her through the doorway crying, 'Wahhh! Mummy,' her face red and covered with food. She is strapped in safe. So she can't climb out and fall on her head.

But what about me? I'm going to crash on the floor. 'Biddy,' I yell. 'Quick! Blow me up again or I'll hit the ground and **burst!**'

But Biddy has forgotten me. She is slip-sliding across the floor to Mum and Dad.

'Is Dad alright?' And, 'Shall I ring the ambulance. I know how to do it—I have to ring **OOO** and say my name, Brigid Lucy. And tell them my address, 13 Haphazard Street . . .'

Mum puts her hand up. 'No, Biddy, darling,' she says, 'but can you please go and comfort Matilda and little Ellen? And walk carefully.' Then reaching up to the POISON—DO NOT TOUCH cupboard, she says, 'I won't be a minute. I'll just get some of Granny's special Rescue Remedy and arnica for Dad's head.'

Biddy smiles and says with her best good girl voice, 'I certainly can,' and walks straight past me to the 'Daddy! Mummy!' crying Matilda.

'What about me?' I yell. 'If I hit the floor I'll be stuck in all that **sticky** bubbly foam and drown to death.'

But Biddy doesn't care.

I start to run. The bubble spins. I'm running inside the bubble, like a mouse in a wheel, spinning it round and round.

And the bubble stops sinking. It floats.
I run and run trying to float the spinning
bubble toward Biddy.

But it's going crooked. Straight towards
Matilda! **Puff**. It bursts on Matilda's arm.
I'm standing on Matilda's arm!

Suddenly she stops crying. She stands
absolutely still, looking at her arm as if she
can feel me.

But then, 'Good stopping crying, Matilda,'
Biddy says, putting her arm around her.

And I quickly run up Biddy's arm and
into her hair. **Safe!**

Me and Biddy are such a good girlfriend
team.

Chapter six

tragic consequences

'It's okay, darling. Daddy is fine,' Biddy says in a mother kind of voice, and we get little Ellen out of her highchair and wipe her face and cuddle her and she stops crying.

Mum puts us all in the bath together. And me and Biddy 'play-very-nicely' with Matilda and little Ellen, even if they only want to play duckies and boring little kids' games like **splashing**.

Now we're finished our bath. Dad is drying and dressing Matilda and little Ellen. So me and Biddy go back to the kitchen. The bubbles are all gone. The floor is clean, the cupboards are all wiped, the dishwasher is silent. **WOW!** The dishwasher washed the dishes and cleaned the whole kitchen.

What a good job done. Mum is going to say we are the best helpers and probably take us to the Botanic Gardens every day to play imaginary princesses.

Where is Mum?

Then we hear Mum talking on the phone. 'Could you come tomorrow?' she says. 'He tries to help but ends up making a **bigger** mess.'

'He' is Biddy's dad. Mum always calls Dad 'he' when he has done something wrong. What has Dad done wrong? We fixed up the not-enough-powder so it can't be that.

'Tonight he put too much powder in the dishwasher.' Mum's voice is **choked** with sadness. 'There was foam all over the kitchen. I had a huge mess to clean up.'

Biddy puts her hand over her mouth. 'But it wasn't Dad. Dad didn't put *enough* powder in. It was me who . . .'

'Don't tell, Biddy,' I say. 'You will get into trouble.'

But she steps forward. 'Mum,' she says.

'Brigid!' Mum says putting her hand up to tell her to be quiet.

'But, Mum,' Biddy says again. 'It wasn't Dad.'

Mum puts her hand over the phone and yells, 'Brigid Lucy. I am on the phone. Please go to bed.'

Biddy twists her mouth sideways to stop herself from talking. Then she goes to wait in the hall for Mum to get off the phone.

We can hear Mum. Talking. Talking. Talking. Then she says, 'Thanks, *Mum*. You are such a help. I'll see you in the morning.'

'Mum?' Biddy whispers. 'Mum said, "Mum". She was talking to Granny!'

Granny is Mum's mum so that is why she calls her 'Mum'. Granny is our absolute favourite grown-up. She's a scientist. She knows everything about magic and nature. She makes all the magic get-well potions for the POISON—DO NOT TOUCH cupboard. And she has all the stories about witches and dragons. She even knows where fairies live.

56

Plus, Biddy can tell her anything. She always sticks up for Biddy, always.

'Mum said, "See you in the morning",' Biddy whispers. 'That means Granny is coming in the morning.'

And so Biddy **forgets** all about telling Mum about the dishwasher. She runs to her room, jumps into bed, pulls the sheet over her head and sings in a whisper, 'Granny's coming over. Granny's coming over!'

Dad comes in to say goodnight. Usually when Dad does the '**goodnighting**', he reads Biddy a story. Then he says, 'Now go to sleep,' turns off the light and goes out. But tonight, he doesn't even open the book.

Biddy puts her arm around Dad and says, 'Daddy, are you alright?'

He nods and opens the book.

'Are you in trouble, Dad?'

Dad smiles a brave smile. 'The dishwasher,' he says.

'Biddy,' I say. 'Don't tell Dad about the dishwasher or we won't get to go to the Botanic Gardens.'

But she doesn't listen.

'But you didn't put too much powder in,' she says. 'You didn't put *enough* in. I had to put more in to make it work.'

'**You what?**' Dad says.

'Stop, Biddy!' I yell, running out to the end of her nose with my arms up. 'Adults can't understand explanations.'

But Biddy explains to Dad about the 'not enough powder'. And how she knows she's not allowed in the POISON—DO NOT TOUCH cupboard. So she used detergent instead.

'But you promised to be **good**,' Dad shouts. 'We shook hands on it! You said you would help.'

'But I was helping,' Biddy says.

'Helping?' Dad says getting up. 'Putting dishwashing detergent in the dishwasher isn't helping!'

Then he glares at Biddy.

'We won't be going to the Botanic Gardens after this,' he says and walks out closing Biddy's door with a **thump**.

I want to tell Biddy, 'I told you not to tell him!' And, 'Why don't you ever listen to me?' But Biddy is so sad, she is not even sucking her thumb. She is just looking at the ceiling, her eyes all crumpled up with **melancholy**. (That's a fairy story word meaning too, too, too sad.)

She is as melancholy as a tristeelia. They are the saddest creatures in the known universe. They come from the Great Bushland where I come from. They live in old cars and tyres that humans have abandoned.

I feel like a tristeelia too. It is like everything is too hard and too sad. I don't know how to help Biddy. So I just lie on her eyelids to make them **heavy**. Then stroke them to make her go to sleep.

Chapter seven

a friendship spell

The next morning we smell cinnamon and dates. 'Granny's porridge,' Biddy says. She jumps out of bed and runs to the kitchen. And there is Granny. Stirring a pot of porridge. 'Granny,' Biddy whispers so she doesn't wake up anyone else, and wraps her arms around Granny's waist.

'How is my **gorgeous** girl?' Granny says. She sits down at the kitchen table and pulls Biddy onto her lap.

Biddy snuggles into her softness for ages and ages. Then she sits up.

'Granny, I'm so glad you are here,' Biddy says. 'The terriblest things have happened. I haven't got one single friend. **No one** at school likes me.' Then Biddy's voice cracks with crying. 'I'm the most all alone no friend person in the entire **universe**.'

'Give it time,' Granny says cuddling her. 'You will find a friend.'

'I was going to get a friend at the Botanic Gardens,' Biddy sobs. 'Now Mum and Dad won't let me go!' She looks up at Granny. 'Please can you make Mum take me to the Botanic Gardens?'

'No, darling,' Granny says, cuddling Biddy closer. 'Your mum is the boss of you. You have to do what she says.'

'But what if *you* tell her, Granny? You are Mum's mum,' Biddy says. 'She has to do what her mum says too.'

Granny laughs. Her whole face **wobbles** with **giggles**, especially her chins. 'Come on now, my clever little one,' she says. 'Let's have our porridge and a nice talk before those noisy babies wake up.'

But then, 'Mummy!' Matilda does wake up and makes so much noise that she wakes up Mum *and* little Ellen.

Then all the time is taken up with changing of nappies, and making of cups of tea and feeding little Ellen porridge.

And Mum is talking to Granny about grown-up stuff like being sick and babies and **hospitals**.

We can't cuddle Granny because Miss Getting-All-The-Attention Matilda has taken up all the space on Granny's knee.

And we can't talk to her because Mum is telling Granny that Biddy is disobedient and **rambunctious**. (Which is like yelling and jumping and having too much fun.) And, 'That-child-will-be-the-death-of-me.'

But Granny doesn't tell Mum off for 'telling tales'. Which is not fair. When Biddy tells tales, Granny says, 'Don't tell tales. Tails are for monkeys.'

That afternoon, when Mum and Matilda and little Ellen lie down to have a rest, me and Biddy get Granny all to ourselves again.

'Granny,' Biddy asks, 'do you really think I will get a best girlfriend?'

'Of course, darling,' Granny says. 'A **wonderful**, kind, clever girl like you will always find a best friend.'

'Can I have a friend, too?'

That's Matilda. She's one of the little kids. She should be sleeping.

So Biddy says, 'Matilda, go back to bed.'

But Granny cuddles Matilda and says, 'I think we need a friendship **spell**.'

'What's a spell?' Matilda asks.

'A spell makes wonderful things happen,' Granny says.

'Like a **miracle**,' Biddy explains to Matilda. 'Can you really make a girlfriend spell?' Biddy asks Granny. 'Can I have a friend with long brown hair in plaits and a pony? Can her name be Isolde?'

'Me too,' Matilda says. 'And a silver grey Siamese cat.'

'No, Matilda,' Biddy says. 'You are too little for making spells.'

But Granny says, 'Actually, **three** people will make the spell stronger.'

'Okay then, Matilda,' Biddy says, 'but you have to do everything Granny says.' She lifts her finger like Mum does when she is very serious. 'No crying or the spell might go wrong and turn you into a frog.'

'I won't cry,' Matilda says and holds her lips tightly together.

'Cat-a-clys-mic Cat-astro-phe!' I say. Spells are real. They are like the Incantation Songs the magical creatures in the Great Bushland use to turn you into a piece of infinity. Remember in Cinderella how the fairy godmother turned the pumpkin into a golden carriage? That's a spell. Or when the wicked witch turned the prince into a frog? They really work!

If Granny casts a spell, Biddy will really get a human friend. 'I've got to **stop** them,' I say running up and down Biddy's arm in panic.

Chapter eight

Diligamus nos salutat

'We need herbs,' Granny says, taking Biddy and Matilda by the hand. 'We need yarrow, some dandelion, a couple of sprigs of lavender . . .'

'Yarrow? Dandelion?' I stop running and **laugh** with relief. Herbs are not spells. Herbs are for potions like the ones in the POISON—DO NOT TOUCH cupboard. The ones Granny makes to fix headaches or bruises or stop people sneezing. Granny's just calling it a spell as an imagination game. What **fun**.

We search for herbs in the front garden and down the street. But all we see is cut-flat lawns and pruned-straight trees and concrete paths.

Until, 'Is this a magic spell-making herb?' Matilda asks picking a daisy.

'Yes!' Granny says. 'Daisies are full of **sunshine**.'

'Here's some more,' Biddy picks four daisies from under Jamie's fence where the lawnmower can't reach.

Granny crouches down. 'Here is some yarrow,' she says. 'There is some lavender. Now where are the dandelions?'

'Is this dandelion?' Biddy says pointing to some tiny yellow flowers struggling up in the crack in the footpath.

'Yes,' Granny says. 'That's all we need.'

When we get home, Granny pops all the herbs in a muslin bag.

'Do we need a **lizard's tail?**' Biddy asks.

'Do you have one?' Granny says.

'Yep, he left his tail in my bedroom when he got a fright,' Biddy says.

'And I've got a **stiff frog**,' Matilda says. 'It came inside and dried up in my room.'

'Well, lizards' tails and frogs are very useful for changing-spells,' Granny says. 'And getting a friend is a change, isn't it?'

Granny drops the lizard's tail and the dried-up frog into the bag.

'Do we have to say special words with the spell?' Biddy asks.

'We will do it tonight,' Granny says. 'Spells work better at night when everyone is **asleep**.'

Which is true. All the magical creatures in the Great Bushland sing their magical Incantation Songs at night. That is why you have to be careful at night-time. If one of their Incantation Songs accidentally rebounds and hits you, it can **zap** you and make you sick or dead. I shiver thinking about the Great Bushland Songs. But this is not a real one. It is just a lizard's tail, dried-up frog and daisies potion. It isn't scary at all.

After dinner, Granny, Biddy and me and Matilda go into Biddy's room. Granny puts the pretend spell bag on the floor and we stand around it in a circle. 'Hold hands,' Granny says. 'Close your eyes. And repeat after me: Let us greet and **love** each other,' she sings in a soft voice.

'What are you doing?' I ask. 'Why are you singing?' Potions don't have singing. Spells and Incantation Songs have singing. '**Stop!**' I yell.

But they don't stop. Biddy and Matilda copy Granny's words carefully.

If they make a proper spell Biddy will get a human friend. I've got to stop it working.

They are holding hands. Dad and Biddy held hands to bind their promise. Maybe if I break the bond between their hands, it will wreck the spell. I race down and squeeze myself between Granny's and Biddy's hands and push. And push. And **PUSH!**

But their hands stay tight together. And Granny continues singing the Spell Incantation Song. '**Diligamus nos salutat**,' she says.

I tickle Biddy on the palm. Perhaps if I can make her palm itchy she will have to let go to scratch it.

But she just frowns and holds on tighter, still repeating Granny's words exactly. '*Diligamus nos salutat.*'

Nothing is working! Biddy is going to get a boring human best friend and I will get eaten by the best friend's cat!

'Let us accept and love each other,' Granny sings.

What about Matilda?

She felt me when me and the bubble landed on her. Perhaps I can make her break the spell. I dive between Biddy's and Matilda's hands and **tickle** Matilda's palm.

She smiles, opens her eyes and looks at Biddy but she keeps holding her hand and repeats Granny's words correctly.

Nothing is working. And Granny keeps singing: '*Esto et diligamus.*'

So, I bite Matilda's palm.

She frowns.

Then I bite and pinch her and bite her again in the soft skin between her fingers.

'Biddy, stop it!!' Matilda yells, letting go of Biddy's hand. 'Stop **pinching** me.'

'I didn't!' Biddy says, scratching her palm.

'What is the matter?' Granny asks. She lets both their hands go and stops singing.

Yes. The Spell Incantation Song is broken. **Whew!**

'You ruined the spell!' Biddy yells.

'I did not! You did!'

'The spell will still work,' Granny says.

Which is a total fib. It takes a long time to make an Incantation Song.

I've heard them making Incantation Songs in the Great Bushland. They sing the words over and over. **Sometimes all night**. Granny didn't even get the whole spell said once.

But Granny doesn't care. She says, 'Come on, off to bed,' and picks up the spell bag and tosses it on the dressing table. 'Spells work best when you are **asleep**.'

Biddy lies in bed whispering, 'I'm going to get a magic miracle girlfriend,' over and over. She only stops when Granny climbs in to sleep in her spare bunk bed and says, 'Shh, now, darling. Goodnight, Biddy.'

I'm so exhausted. I drag myself into Biddy's hair, make a quick hair nest and fall fast asleep.

Chapter nine

a worried anxious night

In the middle of the night Dad comes into Biddy's room to wake up Granny. 'It's started,' he whispers.

'Oh, **good**,' Granny says and gets up.

'What's the matter?' Biddy asks.

'Go back to sleep, darling,' Granny says. 'Everything is alright.'

But Mum and Dad never wake up in the middle of the night unless Matilda or little Ellen is crying. Something is **wrong**.

Biddy thinks so too. She opens her bedroom door and sneaks down the hall to have a look.

I stand on top of her head holding a piece of her hair for balance, my mouth closed tight to see and hear better.

We peek into the lounge room. Mum is frowning and walking and frowning and holding her belly. She looks **sick**.

Dad is saying, 'Are you alright?' and 'What can I do?'

Granny is rubbing Mum's back and sponging her head.

'Mum is sick,' Biddy whispers. 'But Mum never gets sick.'

Biddy is right. Mum never gets sick. Why would she get sick now?

The **spell!**

What if, when I stopped the Spell Incantation Song, it rebounded and accidentally hit Mum? Now she is going to get sick and it is going to be all my fault.

'It's my fault,' Biddy says. 'Mum said I would be the death of her.'

She covers her face with her hands. 'Just because you want a best friend, Brigid Lucy,' she says. 'You did **rudeness**, and arguing and telling tales to Granny. Now Mum is going to die.' She runs to her room, climbs into bed and hides under the sheet.

I want to tell Biddy it wasn't her that made Mum sick, it was me and the rebounding Incantation Song. But I'm so **anxious** and **worried** I can't move.

But we can't stay in the bedroom. We have to sneak down the hall again and again. But no matter how many times we look, Mum doesn't get any better. She walks and sits. She breathes and leans on the wall. She frowns, walks and sits. She breathes and screws up her face and holds her belly.

It is so scary that me and Biddy run back to her bed and curl into a little ball wanting to disappear into ourselves **forever**.

Then Dad comes in. Biddy closes her eyes and pretends to be asleep, so he can't tell her off for making Mum sick.

But he just says, 'Shh, darling,' and picks her up and carries her out to the car.

Mum is in the front seat, but her eyes are closed.

At the hospital, Dad makes beds for Biddy, little Ellen and Matilda on the chairs in the waiting room. Matilda and little Ellen are fast asleep but me and Biddy are just pretending.

Mum is in a room. Every time the door opens you can hear machines **beeping** and **honking**.

First Granny sits with us while Dad goes in with Mum for ages. Then Dad sits with us while Granny goes in with Mum for more ages.

Then Granny comes out and Dad goes in.

Then Dad comes out and Granny goes in.

The nurses rush in and out. Their shoes **squeak** as they walk, just like the hospital on the TV where people die dead.

I know all about deadness. There is lots of it in the Great Bushland where I come from. But we don't have hospitals, so this is a bit different.

Then Matilda rolls over, nearly falls off her chair bed and starts to cry.

'**Shh, shh**,' Dad says picking her up. 'Go back to sleep. Everything's okay.' He lays her across his lap, patting her back.

Matilda snuggles back to sleep.

But me and Biddy know that everything is not okay. The weight of knowing it is so heavy on us we can hardly breathe.

We have to do something to stop Mum dying.

Biddy thinks so too. She crosses her fingers, and her legs and **whispers**, 'Please, fairy godmother, don't let my mum die. I will . . .' She opens her eyes trying to think what she could give up. It would have to be something really big. 'I will give up a best friend,' she says. Then she realises that might not be big enough. She says, 'And I will stop sucking my thumb.'

A panic ripples through her body. But she clenches her fist with the sucking thumb on the inside and whispers, 'I will **never** suck my thumb again.'

Chapter ten
then a miracle happens

'Biddy, are you alright?' Dad asks her.

Biddy sits up. 'Is Mum going to die?'

'No, darling,' Dad laughs. 'She's having a baby.'

'A baby! **Why?**'

'Brigid,' Dad says, 'we told you Mum was having another baby.'

'But that was ages ago. I thought that was Ellen.'

'No, this is another baby.'

'But we don't need another baby,' Biddy says. 'We've already got Matilda and Ellen. That is already **too many**.'

Dad laughs. 'I know, darling, but we're getting another one anyway.'

Biddy stands up, her face serious. 'Dad.

It's not funny. You've got to give it back!'

'Brigid Lucy!' Dad says shocked. 'A baby is a **miracle**.'

'A miracle?' Biddy asks. 'You mean a magic miracle? Like a magic spell miracle?'

'I suppose so,' Dad says.

'No way,' Biddy says looking around for Granny. 'Granny?' she yells

'Brigid sit down and be quiet,' Dad says in an angry whisper.

'But, Dad, I've got to tell Granny before it is too **late**,' Biddy says. 'It was supposed to be a best friend, not a baby.'

'Brigid Lucy!' Dad says. 'Come back here right now.' But he can't get up because Matilda's asleep on his lap.

Biddy knows she should do what Dad says. But this is an **emergency**. So she has to pretend she can't hear Dad. She runs through the doors to Mum's room yelling 'Granny,' ducking under trolleys and between legs. 'Granny.'

It smells in here and there are machines

buzzing and loud breathing noises.

'**Waaaah!**' There's a baby crying.

Biddy sees Granny's legs and pulls at her dress.

'Granny, we made a mistake. We did the miracle spell wrong. We're not getting a best friend. We're getting a baby.'

Granny turns around and laughs. 'Biddy!' She puts her arm around Biddy and brings her in close.

And there on the bed behind her is Mum.

And on Mum's belly is a little fat red baby. He is so tiny and red and crunched up with **squashedness**. He is kicking his little legs and arms and snuggling into Mum's belly.

'Hello,' Biddy says.

And the baby opens his little not-seeing-very-well eyes and looks around. He is trying to find where the voice is coming from.

'This is your little baby brother,' Mum says, her voice all croaky.

'Is he **ours**?' Biddy asks, and reaches out to touch the baby's hand.

The little baby grabs her finger! Biddy laughs and laughs.

I run down Biddy's arm to touch him. His hand is warm and soft and he smells so fresh and new, like a just-opened **butterfly**. I love him. I want to snuggle into his softness and stay there forever.

'So you weren't sick and dying!' Biddy says. 'You mean it wasn't me "being the death of you"?'

'Biddy,' Mum says cuddling her close, 'you knew we were having a baby.'

'But I thought . . .' Biddy says. Then she realises that Mum was never sick and dying. And it wasn't her fault. So she **doesn't** have to give up sucking her thumb. She undoes her fist and releases her sucking thumb. And when she leans on the bed, she holds her sucking thumb right next to her mouth.

Then 'Brigid!' Dad calls from the door. 'Brigid Lucy!'

88

'Go on, darling,' Mum says. 'You'd better go and help Dad with Matilda and little Ellen.'

Dad doesn't tell Biddy off. He just takes her hand and they go back to sit on the chairs next to Matilda and little Ellen. They are still fast asleep.

Biddy climbs up next to Dad and gives him a **hug**. 'Don't worry, Dad. I think this baby will be much better than the last one,' she tells him. 'At least this time it's a boy one. That's a difference.'

Dad laughs and hugs her.

'Can we call him Isolde, Dad?' she asks then changes her mind. 'No, Isolde is a girl's name. What about Isaac? Then he could be a **knight**. Sir Isaac Augustus.'

And we did. We called him Wilfred Isaac Augustus Lucy.

Me and Biddy did miss out on going to the Botanic Gardens. But that was okay because Granny stayed with us for ages and ages and took me and Biddy and Matilda to the **movies**. Me and Biddy and Matilda are kind of friends now because we are the big girls. And it is little Ellen who is the Miss Getting-All-The-Attention little girl and baby Wilfred Isaac who is the Crybaby. So the spell did work for Matilda. And I suppose it did work for me and Biddy too because Biddy didn't get a best human girlfriend. Me and her just lived **happily** ever after.

Epilogue

Except one day when we visit Mum and baby Wilfred Isaac Augustus at the hospital there is **another** family visiting their new baby. And that family has a girl the same age as Biddy.

They smile at each other. Her name is **Ingrid**. She has long hair. But she doesn't have a cat. Biddy wants her to be her forever best friend. And she nearly was. But guess what?

Ingrid invites me and Biddy to come to the zoo with her. Well, she just invites Biddy but I come too. We have the best fun. We eat chocolates and ice-creams. Ingrid's mum doesn't know about preservatives or food colouring.

And me and Biddy and Ingrid run faster than the lion. And do tricks with a huge orangutan. And we feed an armadillo inside the cage! And guess what? Ingrid's mum has the **loudest** scream ever. Nearly louder than a slivigool's. But now, the most splendiferous, fantasmagorical thing in the whole universe is happening. See over there, that big and beautiful lake with a giant fast-asleep-but-not-really crocodile lying on the shore. Well, me and Biddy are going to . . . **OOPS** . . . I'm not allowed to tell anyone.

No, I can't. We will get into trouble.

Okay . . . maybe later. Sorry, this book is full.

So see you later.

Bye!

Magical creatures

Fillikizard dragons —danger rating— tremendously acutely high

Fillikizard dragons are small crocodile-like creatures that have a frill of armour around their necks. They are very powerful hunters. Their back legs spin around like wheels, so they can run terribly fast. They have such huge mouths, they can eat other creatures twice their size. Never try to capture a fillikizard dragon, because they can kill you dead with a blast of their foul breaths from three metres away. If you are too big for them to swallow up, they will slobber all over you and you will stink forever.

Nefariouses—danger rating—tremendously acutely high

Nefariouses are beautiful ancient female beings made entirely of grumpy-and-annoyedness. They live inside the bark of trees. They like absolute silence, so they can make up their evil poems and spells in peace. They have been known to eat noisy children. If you find yourself in a quiet place, never, ever make noise just for fun.

The nefarious who made that silence will gobble you up dead.

Slivigools—danger rating—tremendously acutely high

Slivigools are extremely beautiful and fun-loving beings. They have special nostrils that allow them to breathe underwater and in the air. They love to study their reflections in the water, to comb their long hair, and to play among the pink, waving roots of paperbark trees. But they are very private and hate anyone looking at them. If you stare at them they will scream an ear-piercing scream until they knock you out, and then they will wrap their hair around your legs and drown you to death.

Tristeelias—danger rating—very low

Tristeelias are teeny little creatures with huge sharp teeth and great big eyes so they can see in the dark. They are the saddest creatures in the world. They live in old cars and tyres that humans have abandoned in the Great Bushland. Their job is to chew them up and swallow them to make them disappear. Tyres and cars taste disgusting and make them sick. And they never have any fun ever.

Scoriaks—danger rating—very high

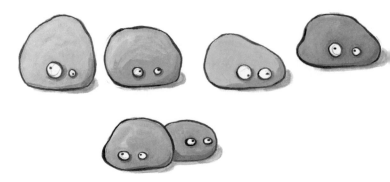

Scoriaks are big, heavy, male creatures that live inside rocks. They are so old that they came into being before the earth began. Their favourite hobbies are sleeping and thinking. If you make a noise and wake them up, they will growl and rumble, and split the earth open. Then they will swallow you whole. Or, if they are too lazy to split the earth open, they will turn you into a piece of infinity with just one look of their evil eyes. Be extremely careful when you move rocks around. Sit beside the rocks first to see if you can hear a soft snore. If you can, back away very quietly and go and find another rock to move.

Magical swearwords

Cat-a-clys-mic Cat-astro-phe!
Fan-tas-mag-or-ical

Magical spell words

Garrlim.
Gooolim.
Ambidextrous.
Pyrotechnics.

Look out for . . .

When Biddy's pet slug has a terrible
accident, Dad buys Biddy a pet goldfish
called Rolly Polly.

    The invisible imp that lives in Biddy's
hair thinks Rolly Polly is boring.

    But then Biddy trains Rolly Polly to do
tricks . . . and it's not long until things start
to go wrong.

Look out for . . .

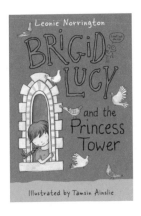

Biddy is excited when she spots a real-life Princess Tower from the window of the train. So is the invisible imp that lives in Biddy's hair.

Mum says the tower is a cathedral, but what do grown-ups know?

When Biddy and the imp investigate further, they discover that Princess Rapunzel is trapped inside the tower.

Can Biddy save the day?

Acknowledgements

To the Tasmanian Writers' Centre, for giving me a residency in their wonderful Hobart studio where, trying to blend in with this old world and beautiful city, my little imp got me into lots of delicious trouble. To Libby and Margrete, for generously inviting me to join their table, which led to our friendship and working relationship. And, most importantly, to my niece, Brigid Tony Izod, who inspired the character Brigid Lucy.